Federico Ivanier is an acclaim
young people. He has written ov
been published across Latin An
occasion, his works have been a
for Literature from the Uruguayan Ministry for Education
and Culture as well as the Premio Bartolomé Hidalgo, one
of the country's most important literary awards. Federico
has also worked occasionally as a screenwriter and teaches
English as a second language.

Claire Storey translates from Spanish and German into
English. She specialises in literature for younger readers
with a particular interest in MG and YA fiction. In 2021/22,
she was given funding from Arts Council England for a
translation project focusing on Young Adult Literature
from Latin America. She regularly volunteers in schools
to talk about careers with languages and was named
Outreach Champion 2021 by the Institute of Translation
and Interpreting.

NEVER TELL ANYONE YOUR NAME

FEDERICO IVANIER

Translated by Claire Storey

HopeRoad Publishing
PO Box 55544
Exhibition Road
London SW7 2DB

www.hoperoadpublishing.com
First published in Great Britain by HopeRoad in 2023
Copyright © 2020 Federico Ivanier

Translation (c) Claire Storey

This work has been published within the framework of the
IDA Translation Support Programme.

ISBN 978-1-913109-22-6
eISBN 978-1-913109-31-8

Printed and bound by Clays Ltd Elcograf S.p.A

For Ana

1

And this is how you open your eyes, slowly, enjoying the movement of the train, even though you have no clue where you're going. For a second you prefer to think you don't know anything; it's a moment to start over again, an instant when you're someone else. It's a second of nothingness, perfect innocence that stretches infinitely, so far that you're swimming in it, submerged and happy.

Because, after all, where are you?

You were dreaming. You remember that much, albeit somewhat vaguely. That's how dreams disappear; gradually, like a mirage on the highway. But anyway, you know all too well what the apparition in your mind was about: the same ghost as always. You were dreaming of Lucrecia's heavenly eyes. On repeat. You're still dreaming of her, even though you should have forgotten her by now. Your brain continues to function beyond your control; you keep telling it to forget her, but it ignores you. It floats off and remembers.

The calm of rest is over. You're fully awake now. And the distance comes back to you: she, Lucrecia, an ocean away. She, Lucrecia, beyond the Atlantic. She, Lucrecia, in Montevideo. Or so you presume. She, Lucrecia, six thousand five hundred miles away.

Six thousand five hundred miles. A distance you struggle to even imagine. A distance impossible to feel with your senses, a crushing, inhuman distance. Even so, it's closer than the distance she put between you when she said, 'It's over,' three weeks ago, the night before you left for France. Seven letters, pronounced in a single second, more powerful than the following twelve hours on the plane. Seven letters more powerful than those six thousand five hundred miles.

Lucrecia, the girl with the white T-shirt, heavenly eyes, long hair and denim shorts. Almost a cliché. A girl like a photo in a rock video, like a character in a road movie, hitching a ride in the middle of the desert. Lucrecia, who wasn't angry or sad when she told you. You'd been expecting it, however much you tell yourself otherwise. And although you never wanted that moment to arrive, it did, and there's nothing you can do about it. You didn't do anything then, and you still don't know if you can do anything now. You didn't even reply, protest, or stand up to her. You just let it happen. She gave you a piece of paper with a hand-written poem on it, told you those two words and then disappeared. A poem and a goodbye.

2

And you? You just stood there. Watching her. Letting it all happen.

You have to get used to how things are now that Lucrecia's no longer there. You have to get used to it and you know it. But it's going to be difficult if you keep dreaming about her. For three weeks you've been saying, 'Don't do it, don't do it,' over and over, as if you could control your dreams. Or your feelings. Three weeks of the same thing. All the time you were in Bordeaux. And the worst thing is that you knew, you *knew* the thing with Lucrecia wouldn't end well. You knew it since that night at the party, on that sofa, while Catupecu was playing on the stereo. You can't give yourself the luxury of dreaming about her. You knew it then and you know it now, on the train en route to Madrid. But your head dreams whatever it likes.

You look out of the window, a sea of rails beyond it, criss-crossing, meeting, separating, and coming back together again further on, weaving a vast and complex braid. Freight wagons, robust and dented, appear and disappear in front of your window. *You are now arriving into Hendaye*, the loudspeaker on the train announces. About to cross the border from France into Spain.

The train, which had already slowed down, now stops completely. You stay sitting a moment longer. You watch the rest of the passengers collect their luggage and disembark, brief conversations among themselves. French resonates in your ears. You think of it as the language of

3

love (another cliché), and yet you still can't understand it properly; it's as if you have a mental block. Even though you've been studying it for three years, even though you've just spent three weeks in the country, the sounds remain a mystery. A mass of melodic echoes, like purring kittens. You understand individual words, but you can't grasp the full meaning, you miss the important bits. Your brain's a sieve.

You humph. You want to stay in your seat. You feel a headache coming on around the back of your head. You have to stand up, but you want to stay sitting down. You're too comfortable. And tired, although you're not sure why. It's as if you're recovering from a fever, a fever you never had, one that never fully arrived. You're only sixteen, so how can you feel so tired? It's ridiculous, but you're worn out. For no good reason, but you're exhausted all the same. You're hungry, that must be it.

Inside the train, the temperature feels pleasant. It all seems pleasant, as if the world is perfect. But it's not. Outside, waiting patiently, lies the anger of a leaden sky. Its apathy cold and windy. Angry and apathetic, is it possible to experience two contradictory feelings at the same time? Clearly the sky can. You lean back and relax, breathing calmly. If you close your eyes, you'll see Lucrecia again, smiling that smile that always drew you in, scarcely moving her pink lips, barely showing her teeth. Yes, Lucrecia smiling at you, and, for a second, looking at you. Her full

4

attention on you and you alone. You'd only be imagining her, of course. But you're fed up with imagining, so you keep your eyes open, wide open.

You turn to look outside again, towards the world of tracks: steel on wood, wood on stone, stone on stone. The train moves again, covering the short distance to reach Irun, the Spanish side of the border, and your face floats in the glass window, a ghost above the rails. Your double, looking in from outside. As a boy, you used to question whether there was someone out there who looked identical to you, and if there were, what kind of life did they lead? This idea stuck with you after reading Mark Twain's *The Prince and the Pauper* where the two characters looked so alike that they swapped lives. And you held on to the fantasy of being someone else, even if just for a while.

You tell yourself it's nothing more than a reflection in the window, turning to face the other side. The loudspeakers announce that you've arrived in Irun and the train pulls to a halt, the brakes squealing. At the front of the carriage, the red numbers on the clock show it's a quarter past three in the afternoon. The other train, the one destined to take you to Madrid, leaves at four.

And so you stand up, pick up your backpack, check your minor's passport and your documents, just in case. Everything's in order to cross the border. You're ready to change trains.

Or so you think.

2

Irun station is a squat building with grey floors, grey walls, grey lighting. The chairs in the waiting rooms are made from polished sleepers placed on steel bases, also grey, that had once been rails. Your perception of it all is automatic. Nobody looks at you, not directly at you, alone in the station, and likewise, you pay no attention to anyone or anything. That's fine. You like to be lost in the masses with nobody knowing you're there.

You take a few steps forward, or rather, you move without really going anywhere, mindlessly. You're swimming in a nebulous sea of faces, necks, luggage, dust. You inhale. Someone smells of garlic, and it turns your stomach. You're not going to stay here long; that would be awful. The place feels depressing, and you're impatient at having to wait. You never were any good at waiting.

You step out onto the platform, ready to climb aboard, but the train waiting for you, a Spanish train, disappoints you. It's nothing like the French one. It's from a different era — the sixties or seventies perhaps — with uncomfortable seats and a mournful appearance. It looks like the bus from that old film your dad made you watch, what was it again? The one with the boy about your age who had the chance to write an article about a rock band for *Rolling Stone*.

He always makes you watch films that for some reason or other he considers good for you. He has a plan, and you accept it; there's no other option. He'd be hurt if you didn't, so you go along with it, even though you're not always that enthusiastic. Your mother, when you speak to her (which isn't very often), has different ideas about what's good for you, and what's not, blah, blah, blah. The two of them try to complement each other, yet they inhabit two parallel worlds that never cross. But essentially they're both just doing the same: trying to pass things on to you that they consider good, to bend you to their tastes.

Almost Famous, that was the film. The character's name was William. And the band, Stillwater. It's incredible how your mind sometimes stores names you swear you don't remember. Stillwater was a really great band, and it was William's job to follow them on tour and get all the insider gossip. While on tour, William met one of Stillwater's groupies, Penny Lane. She was a bit older than him, in her early twenties perhaps, sensual, and problematic. Even though it was obvious their love was doomed from the start, and even though William must have known that, he couldn't stop it from happening.

You think about the film. You think about William aged fifteen. You think that just as he had a zeal for writing, yours is for taking photos. That's what you and he have in common, a passion for keeping records. Beyond simply the thrill of watching the film back then, *Almost Famous* has affected you more than you'd ever admit because it often crosses your mind.

But you didn't get William's life with the beautiful Penny Lane; you got a solo journey on a dilapidated train. That's all. In fact, that's kind of how you see the next few hours of your future: dilapidated. Well, you never did like everything to be perfect, smiling, and unproblematic. It makes you nervous. So with good grace, you accept the imperfect situation you're facing.

Traces of soot accumulate on the unpainted metal of the carriages. The sheen that the surface must once have had is no more than a distant memory that has almost dissipated. It will remain in the most concealed, intimate atoms of the metal, perhaps. You inhale. You still feel as if you're moving in slow motion, as though you're still asleep and dreaming on the other train.

You don't spend much time on the platform. You climb aboard, discreetly fighting against the bodies of the other passengers, invaded by their scent, their body heat, and you can think only of how hungry you are. Inside the carriage, it begins to warm up. The blank screens at either end look like strange antiques, giving the impression they are old black and white TVs. The windows are so low you can only look out of them if you're sitting down. If you stand up, your gaze hits the luggage racks and the ceiling. The leaden light filters through the meagre windows. The train is not due to leave yet.

You struggle to find the seat number on your ticket, the one you bought in France. But you soon find it. Fourteen. You have to bend down to locate it on the seat. You stash your backpack and suitcase up on the luggage racks and sit down, thinking about the hunger in your belly, crouching like a beast gnawing away inside you and opening up an emptiness that's difficult to settle.

You could have bought something at the station; you didn't think about it. But anyway, it wouldn't have resolved the problem, not really. And honestly, even though the journey will take several hours, you can't be bothered to get off the train again. You just want to lean back in your seat, listen to music, clear your mind and try to turn off the stubborn pain in your head that's creeping up from the back.

That's when the girl with glasses and short, blue-dyed hair approaches. You don't see her, not to start with. You're already settled in your seat, scrolling through a playlist your dad sent you before you left. The first song is 'Loving Cup' by the Rolling Stones, and it inevitably makes you think of

Lucrecia. Everything makes you think of Lucrecia, even the music you never even listened to with her, because you'd like to listen to it with her … and you're off, imagining memories with her.

That's why you don't see the girl with glasses, because of the daydream, and the drowsiness that's taken over your body, this immense state of suspension you find yourself in. You only hear her voice speaking with a strong French accent:

'Excuse me, but these are our seats.'

You raise your head, convinced this sentence was aimed at someone else. But no, the girl, who must be a similar age to Penny Lane, is looking at you.

'It can't be,' you reply calmly. You take your ticket out of your pocket and check the seat number. 'Fourteen,' you nod confidently, showing her the printed number. For your own peace of mind, you even check it should be an aisle seat, which is where you're sitting.

'Us too,' the girl replies, showing you the numbers on her ticket.

'Are you in the right car?' you think to ask.

The French girl (you've assumed she's French, but she could be from anywhere) checks. 'Seven,' she says, and then both of you look up at the same time, searching for the plastic sign at the front of the carriage. It says *Coche 7*. You check the number on your ticket, and it too says seven.

You reach the conclusion that they must have sold the same ticket twice, and like the inexperienced traveller you are, you ask yourself what to do in this situation. You tell yourself it would have been easier to fly, but no, you didn't want the easy option, you wanted to travel by train, to see the countryside, breathe in the details, and delay your arrival in Madrid. A stupid whim that your mother decided to indulge because it's better for the environment to travel by train, and besides, since she left for France, she's been far less of a mamá to you than to the twins. But now that whim has brought you here, and somehow, you're going to have to think your way out of this, although you're not entirely sure how.

You come up with the most obvious solution: speak to someone in charge on the train to reassign your seat, but the girl's boyfriend, an intellectual-looking hippie, with seemingly dishevelled hair and beard which are perfectly coordinated with his coconut shell earrings, points to the dates on the tickets. Theirs says the ninth of January; yours, the tenth.

'I think you've got the wrong day,' he says.

'What day is it today?' you ask without lifting your eyes from the tickets.

'The ninth,' replies the girl.

'Not the tenth?'

'No, it's the ninth, Sunday the ninth.'

And so it's nearly four o'clock on Sunday the ninth of January — not the tenth — when you jump off the train and arrive back at the ticket kiosk, asking yourself what could possibly have happened, how could you have got it so wrong? But you don't have an answer, and in any case, what does it matter? The ticket's for the tenth and today is the ninth.

You stand in front of the window. Behind the glass is a fat guy with a beard and a badly knotted tie, devouring a tuna empanada he has next to his computer keyboard. His moustache is so long it's hiding his lips, which makes it look as if the empanada is being plunged into a hole in his skin. A few crumbs get caught in the fine hairs around the hole.

You explain the problem to him and wait to see what he says.

'It's the last day of the holidays, everyone's on their way home,' the fat guy replies — as if you need the explanation — as he swallows a mouthful of empanada and searches for free seats on the computer screen.

'I know,' you say, annoyed because you hate obvious statements. 'I know.'

The fat guy barely raises his eyebrows and keeps looking, taking another bite of the empanada, pressing his lips together as he chews, tilting his head from side to side.

'Fully booked,' he concludes.

You take a deep breath, not replying instantly.

'You have nothing?'

'Absolutely nothing.'

It's strange. On the one hand, the idea of having nothing available today and therefore having no clue about where you're going to spend the night, terrifies you. But on the other hand, you feel nothing. The situation is so unheard of that your directory of feelings and sensations can't find the right file. Maybe that's why you create a picture in your head: being at the border, you imagine yourself lurking in the shadows. The image alarms you, of course, but your curiosity is also piqued.

You could call your parents and ask for help. But you hate the idea of doing that. It would be like admitting defeat, although you can't quite explain why. You scratch your eyebrow and take a second to think. Your headache's intensifying, blending with your hunger. It clouds your judgement a little. You need to eat.

'There's not a single empty seat on this train?'

'The Three Wise Men left on the sixth, chaval,' the fat guy responds, with a sense of humour you don't share. 'It's full, full, not even half a seat.'

The fat guy breathes heavily, and you grimace at the different sounds of the language, his Spanish grating against yours. The words, the phrasing, it all sounds strange and you have to make an effort to keep up with him.

'Nothing?' you ask.

'Nothing. And even if there were, you'd have to pay a supplement.'

'That's not a problem,' you reply.

He sighs again, as if the fact you could pay (and you're so willing to do so) makes his life so much more complicated.

'All the same, it's all full. Holidays are over and everyone's heading home.' He doesn't take his eyes off the screen, almost taking pleasure in it. 'It's all full.'

'Are you sure?'

'Absolutely. And I don't think we've got anything on the special midnight service either. But let me check.'

'What time does it leave?'

'Midnight, like I just said.'

It's not a great solution, but at least it avoids the problem of having to find somewhere to sleep.

'What time does that train arrive in Madrid?' you ask.

'Seven a.m.'

'And is there any space?'

'Vaya!' The fat guy surprises himself, so much that he drops his empanada. 'There's one seat left on the midnight train.'

'Awesome.' You exhale, with obvious relief. 'Can we swap the ticket now?'

When you finish the transaction, there are just two words in your mind: eight hours. Eight hours until midnight and your train. Four hundred and eighty minutes. It's not that long, you tell yourself, resigning yourself to it, although you're convinced that the boredom will kill you. And that's not all. You hate it, but you also know that you have to let your dad know. He's not going to like it. He'll be annoyed with you, and with your mother for not having put you on a plane, even though it was you that bought the ticket.

The best thing would be not to tell him anything, but he's collecting you at Atocha station at the time you will actually now only just be getting on the train. Better to get it over and done with, sooner rather than later, so you call his phone and tell him you'll be arriving by train at seven in the morning.

'Why?' he asks you, worried. 'What happened?'

'Nothing, there was a problem with the French train and I missed the connection to Irun.'

The lie slips out before you notice. It's not particularly believable, you think. It's not the first time you've lied either, but this time feels more justified. You complete it by telling him you've already let your mother know; that'll prevent any arguments between them. Your dad finally accepts you'll be arriving tomorrow, he's more philosophical than you were expecting, after all, it's a time he considers more reasonable than midnight. With that task complete, it's as if a huge hole in time has suddenly opened up, a chasm in an invisible place, and there you are, all alone with those eight hours to kill.

And the first thing you do is look around. You examine the empty station in all its drabness, complete with the fat guy, who's still entertained with his computer screen. Eight hours waiting here will last so long, it'll be unbearable. You turn on your music at random and a version of 'Elevador' by the band Catupecu plays. You wander towards the platform where the train was, the one which has now disappeared as

15

if by magic. You don't even know when it left. You didn't notice.

You look at the tracks, now empty, and you remember that when you were little, you used to enjoy watching the trains, the few times you could. You'd stand next to the tracks, as close as possible, while your dad held onto you. And you'd watch the mass of steel approach. You used to think of trains as giant worms that would come off their tracks and eat you. Nothing new there. You always liked to imagine a world full of monsters.

You know you're going to leave the station to wander around Irun. You're not going to stay here; that was never your plan. You leave your suitcase and your backpack at the storage office in the station. All you take with you is a small bag that you hang over your shoulder. It contains your wallet with all your documents and your camera so you can take some photos or make a video. Whatever you might find to record. All you know is that Irun is your future. And the time has come to meet it.

At the end of the day, wherever you go, you always end up face-to-face with your future.

16

3

January in the Basque Country isn't a particularly friendly month for anyone wanting to walk. You've thought it before and today has confirmed it. You look up and see the clouds pushing across the sky. You don't care. You take out your camera to see what you can find, readjusting your scarf and hat to protect yourself from the cold, and think, 'Bring it on.'

You cross the tracks and try to leave by a side door on the left that is closed for some reason. The door redirects your steps to the other side towards a long iron staircase leading upwards into the unknown.

You go up, step by step, spotting some freight wagons off to one side. Their bellies full of stone and their metallic skin showing signs of rusty knocks and blows. Automatically, you take a photo, recording it on your camera's memory card (it's a semi-professional camera that cost around five hundred euros, sent by your mother to atone for her guilt and to play happy families). The clean air enters your lungs, and you start to feel better as you begin to see the trees and bushes, as you move closer to the sky.

In your earphones, Catupecu's 'Entero o a pedazos' is playing — 'Whole or in Pieces' — but it's the acoustic version. It's as if the guitar, the bass and the violin are taking turns in the boxing ring. When you reach the top of the stairs, you find a main road, with two lanes heading in both directions. Even though it's Sunday and there's not many people about, you're convinced this is the main road; you can go anywhere from here.

You don't have a map. No internet connection. You could get a map at the station, but you don't. You look around. A couple argue next to a stop sign. A boy in a wheelchair strokes a Labrador puppy. A guy wearing headphones rummages through the bins.

You turn left and just as you start walking, you bump into someone. It's a young man, in his early twenties, wearing John Lennon glasses. He makes a gesture of apology and carries on his way. The reflective lenses mean you can't see his eyes, but he smiles as he walks away.

'No problem,' you say, smiling back at him.

You notice something: you're happy. A simple happiness. It occurs to you that this is the best bit of the whole trip: a sigh, a curve, a question mark, a detour, a call to adventure. A little further on, the street dips and on the horizon, you see mountains surrounded by green valleys, their summits hidden by clouds and snow.

You walk. Your head still hurts a little and your stomach is still growling, begging. Hunger's been a problem ever since you met Lucrecia. You rummage in your pockets and find a couple of chocolate-covered raisins. Nothing else. You look in your wallet. After paying the extra fare, there's not much left. You smile to yourself. You're almost like the pauper in Twain's book.

You lift your eyes and sigh. The street is peaceful, almost deserted. You walk along a few hundred metres. The buildings have red roof tiles, with brick or white-painted walls. There are even some made of granite. Nothing higher than five or six storeys. Irun looks clean and orderly, the few cars that drive past are taking their time, even the wind blows meekly.

You try to imagine what it would be like to live here. You observe the closed shops: several clothes shops, a sweet shop, a small bookshop, a stationery shop, a language school. You let yourself be carried along by the breeze. You reach an important junction, a broad expanse leading to the town hall. Several roads converge, edged with yellow and white lines. With the terrace in front of the municipal building, the place feels like a wasteland.

Perhaps in an attempt to fill the space, they've put in a merry-go-round, some swinging chairs, a Ferris wheel (a small one at that) and a cart selling hot chocolate and churros that's closed right now. It makes it feel like a fairground. There's a giant white rabbit, standing alone, with a bucket of coloured plastic bubble wands to sell.

You remember when you were little you were scared of these oversized characters. The rabbit's worn-out costume is coming undone at the seams and you wonder if anybody really believes. Reality filters through the disguise, sneaking in all over. Perhaps when you were little that would have made it even more terrifying. That ragged seam suggesting the person behind the mask doesn't care enough about keeping up appearances. Like they want to make you think they're good and kind, but really, deep down, they don't actually care what you think. As if they know that sooner or later, you'll find out the truth.

On the other hand, it's also true that you don't know and that nobody knows who is inside that costume. So in a way, it works: it maintains the lie. It could literally be anyone. That's why you take their picture. And he — or she — unexpectedly poses.

Nearby is a leftover memory of Christmas: a seven-metre-tall pine tree, the coloured lights still hung, but forgotten already; nobody pays any attention to them. They still flicker tastelessly in the bland Sunday light. Behind the tree there's a red Peugeot flipped on its top, surrounded by yellow police tape. You struggle to imagine how it got like that. Irun doesn't seem like the sort of place for an accident of that scale. You almost believe accidents couldn't possibly happen here. But welcome to what lies beneath those first impressions: the dirty wheels point towards the chalk-white sky; a shower of broken glass is sprinkled across the ground; pieces of paper and an empty packet of M&Ms rest on the car's ceiling. You capture all these details on your camera.

You continue onwards. Your belly growls again. You try to ignore it, wrapping yourself up entirely in your bubble of freedom, a destination-free stroll, purposeless. Your feet tread the wide pavements, your lungs fill with air coming from the leafy borders. You have more than enough time. It's a relief, liberating.

The street grows steeper, and the mountains begin to grow taller, or at least that's how it seems. A few streets further on you reach a square that opens up to your right. The deck chairs wait expectantly, but there's nobody nearby, everything's still. Dotted across the grass are a few brown bushes, willows and birches, skeletal, devastated by winter.

A young couple sits kissing on a bench. A one- or two-year-old grey Weimaraner runs around with its tongue lolling out and ears flapping. The look on its face says it's the best dog in the world. You stretch out your arms and rest them on the back of a chair. The sun filters through the clouds and honestly, you don't need much else. Well, you need to satisfy your hunger, but you force yourself to enjoy the moment all the same and bask in the joy of having nothing to do.

Some long-legged ducks waddle about on the grass not far from you. Their feathers grey on their backs and white on their chests. They waddle around and then some unexpectedly take flight. The Weimaraner follows them, wagging its tail until it's not too far from one of the ducks just behind you. Then it crouches down.

For a moment, the world stops moving, followed by a rapid chase. The dog stretches its muzzle towards the bird. Feathers fly and the bird is trapped in the dog's jaws, wings half open. It looks like a game, but the open beak with the tongue hanging out in desperation is a mute call for help.

The dog doesn't release its prisoner, but doesn't know what to do with it either. It's not hungry, like you; it's just that instinct broke through the comforts of domestic life. So it drops the bird on the ground, smells it, and picks it up again. For a dog, killing is returning home. To what it really is. Now the dog carries the bird towards the couple. The owner stands up to tell the dog to drop it. The dog obeys and the duck remains where it is on the ground, a shapeless mass.

The Weimaraner's looking at the bird and wagging its tail while the owner —who's no more than twenty years old — tells the dog off. On the ground, the wings barely move, only the feathers flutter in the breeze. The duck twitches, face up. It doesn't have long left. And what time is left will be agony. The couple doesn't know what to do. They glance around, clip on the leash and move away quickly, while the beak stays open, gasping for air.

You approach the bird, thinking about killing it to alleviate its suffering, but you don't know how. You can't see any stones and you can't bring yourself to tread on it. You couldn't, even if you wanted to. And you don't want to. You crouch down a little, watching death close-up with a volatile and indefinable sadness. Should you take a picture of this? And then you hear the voice, speaking with a Spanish accent.

'Once a hunter, always a hunter, eh?'

It's a girl. She's on your left, a little further behind you. You didn't see her arrive; you didn't even hear her. You can't sense her. Even now as you look at her from below, she looks like a painting: her silhouette outlined against a tree and the sky. The branches form a crown, the cloud a frozen explosion. Dyed black hair, large eyes, black too. Pink lips, pale, barely distinguishable against her skin. A slender face, a broad forehead. You take in the details as if you're tasting them. The girl smiles. Now you're standing up, the sweet smell of her perfume hits you and almost knocks you out. You understand how the sailors felt when they heard the sirens' songs.

'What?' you ask.

'Weimaraners were hunting dogs,' she explains, like a simple fact of nature. 'That's what they were bred for.'

'I didn't know that.'

'Well, now you do. They're a mixture. Their roots go back to Africa, or Asia. Apparently, they're great for hunting in forests. Or marshland. Or at least they used to be. I guess they probably always will be.'

'Oh,' you say.

'Sorry, I didn't mean to bother you.'

'No, no. You're not bothering me.'

She looks at you with deep, dark eyes, probably trying to locate your accent. Or so you imagine. She seems curious and in no hurry to move on. You can't work out her age — she could be the same age as you, she could be older or even a little younger. No, older. Definitely older. Early twenties. You keep the conversation going; you don't want to be rude.

'I don't know much about Weimaraners.'

'I don't know much either, really. My brother's a vet, all I know is what he's told me. All the different breeds have their own backgrounds, you know. Even if those little doggies look super friendly, to their prey they're still absolute monsters. But people love their pets. Whatever they do, they'll always think they're angels.'

You nod thoughtfully.

'I have a cousin called Ezequiel,' you say, surprising yourself at this memory. 'He never liked dogs until his mom brought home a boxer pup. One day, he had no choice but to take the dog out and tons of girls approached him just to talk about his dog. Or to pet it. Ever since then, he's always taken it out.'

Her lips stretch to a smile. Compact white teeth appear underneath.

'What was the dog called?' she asks you.

24

'Arnold. As in Schwarzenegger.'

The smile stretches wider.

'And did he complain?' she asks.

'What about?'

'That he was being taken out for walks just to attract the girls?'

'No, not so far anyway. I guess he's happy.'

'I can imagine.'

Suddenly, you catch her looking at you. You try to hold her gaze, and once again you wonder how to keep the conversation going. You hate how inexperienced you are at all this.

'What about you? Didn't you ever have a dog to take out on the pull?' she asks you.

She seems interested in chatting with you. You're surprised. And pleased. And in the middle of it all, you find the phrase 'on the pull' funny. It makes you think of someone being dragged along by the dog. You can't imagine how that would help make you attractive to girls.

'No,' you smile. 'I don't have a dog. I never had one. But I once heard on TV about some study in England that said people who own dogs are healthier, happier and live longer. Maybe that's why, because they take you out to walk and meet people.'

'The English carry out a lot of ridiculous studies. The other day I read they were doing one to find out why girls like pink.'

'What was the conclusion?'

'Well apparently, women used to go out to pick fruit and they must have had a particular sense for knowing when the fruit was ripe. As the ripe fruit tended to be red, girls now like pink.'

'And is it true?'

'Well, I don't like pink, I can tell you that much. Right, well …' The girl sighs. 'Okay, have a lovely day.'

You did something wrong, you think to yourself. Your stomach suddenly starts to hurt as you see she's now disappearing, just as easily as she arrived.

'Thanks. You too,' you reply.

She turns, smiling as she leaves. You have a better view of her now, you can watch her at your leisure. Slim, tight-fitting clothing, gloves, scarf around her throat.

'I hope so,' she responds, and leaves.

On the ground, the duck is dead.

4

Time drags by. For a few moments, you stay where you are, disappointed because the girl's gone so quickly. You decide to walk on. You roam the streets, up and down, wandering aimlessly. The mountains make you feel that the closer you get to them, the further away they are. It's a strange effect, a perspective that's difficult to define.

Up above, the felt clouds are starting to fray and behind them emerges a hazy colour, orange and violet. You reach a stream of flat, muddy water flowing through the centre of Irun. It bends and curves, but its brown current is weak, barely moving, confined within the walls of stone and concrete.

You're in a residential area, surrounded by apartment blocks. Nearby, there's an overgrown plot and you spy an enormous house, three storeys high, emerging from the vegetation. The central part has been almost completely destroyed; it's just about held together by some thick steel beams. You take photo after photo, thinking that you must look like a tourist and wondering if this is in any way risky, you know, being alone and all that. Finally, you look back over your photos: some from Montevideo where you live, some from Bordeaux with your mother and her family. Because you can't help but see it that way. As a family that isn't yours. Not truly.

Little by little, night falls. The streetlights come on, their balls of light a golden glow. The sky turns a deep purple and a cold wind picks up, penetrating the weave of your clothes. You sigh as your feet continue their random steps. Since Lucrecia, you get bored easily.

You reach an old chapel. A giggling child is skipping along dressed as Death, all in black, with a mask and a cardboard scythe. A woman follows behind carrying a present. You focus your lens carefully. Filling the frame, the boy seems genuinely threatening, reaping lives. For a while you follow the path traced by mother and child, parallel to the stream, allowing them to guide you. You cross one of the many small bridges, which leads you out into the Plaza Mayor, the main square. Here too, the lamps begin to light up and in turn, doors and windows spill light onto geranium-decorated balconies. Beneath them are seats filled with people chatting, laughing, eating.

And there's the church that the people of Irun surely consider the most important one. It's a place where you can sit down, that can shelter you from the wind. So you climb the steps, cross the broad foyer and enter the main chamber.

A priest is at the altar, speaking to some parishioners gathered towards the front. Off to one side, you see a smiling photograph. You can't make it out properly, but then again, you're not really paying attention. Underneath the photo is a flower arrangement. You hang back, unsure of your own movements. Is it okay to come in? Are you interrupting something private? The warm air settles it for you. You're not being disrespectful to anyone by warming up a little.

There are quite a few people, and gas heaters are located in the corners of the central nave. So you sit down, well back on the left. The words spoken at the front become a murmur. You think you hear something about somebody who died a little while ago.

You close your eyes and your body lets out a sigh of relief and satisfaction. The pain in your head's still there, but that's all. It's trying to clamber from the nape of your neck up to the rest of your head. And the hunger, of course. That hunger you're trying to ignore.

You breathe deeply. You turn on your phone, searching through the classics on your reading app until you find the one you want, and you start to read. You try to concentrate, but you're distracted by the scent of a perfume you recognise. You tilt your head slightly, and you see the girl you met by the dead duck walking down the central aisle.

And just as you expect her to keep walking forward, she turns to the side where you are. She sees you and, for an incredible instant, your eyes meet hers and neither of you look away. You're sure that normally you would look the other way. But not today. This time you want to look at her, so you do. She looks back at you, her eyebrows raised. And she walks towards you.

'Hello. You're here?' she whispers.

'Yes,' you reply, as if you were doing something naughty. But this time, that feeling fades away. Her perfume crashes over you like waves. You can't work out exactly what it smells of. Flowers, but you couldn't say which ones. A million different flowers. Something sweet, but not sickly. You've been surprised by your sense of smell. It's no longer under your control as much.

'I came here … to rest a while.'

She turns forward. She looks like she's thinking about what to do, which catches you off guard; she doesn't seem like a girl who spends a lot of time thinking about what to do.

Once again, as if on loop, you wonder if you should suggest a topic of conversation. Shouldn't you at least ask about the person that died? Maybe she knew them and that's why she's here. But you doubt it. Then again, nobody goes to a church just to chat. Do they?

So you revert back to that same plan of action as in the train station: you wait. You wait and wait and wait. And wait a little more. In reality, every time you wait, you're getting better at it. And anyway, there's no rush. You like the presence of this girl by your side. It soothes you. And that's why you can wait. You can wait as long as you need to.

She sits down, keeping her eyes forward. Out of the corner of your eye, you glance over her profile, overlaid against a backdrop of painted angels — both earthly and heavenly — on the opposite wall of the church. A picture within a picture.

'You're Argentinian, aren't you?'

'No. Uruguayan.'

'Ah, *uruguasho*.'

Her pronunciation, forced and mocking, sounds fake, and funny. It makes you smile, putting you in a good mood. You feel optimistic again.

'Yes, *uruguaio*,' is your response, putting on a false Spanish accent to counter her Uruguayan one. For a moment, you both stop, and everything becomes a photo image, imprinted in the hidden camera in your brain: her lips stretched to a smile, her pronounced cheekbones, the shine gleaming from her eyes.

'Well,' continues the girl, 'you've all got the same accent down there, haven't you?'

'No.'

She looks at you as if she's expecting you to go on, but you have little else to say. In the end, she just smiles thinly. Another smile you find hard to stop watching, that you're sad to see go.

'So? What were you just doing?' she asks.

You show her your phone.

'Reading.'

'Reading what?'

'*Dracula*.'

'*Dracula*?!'

'Yes.'

'In a *church*?!'

'It's a classic.'

'Yeah, but come on, vampires, *here* …?'

'What's wrong with that?'

'The Prince of Darkness in the middle of a church? You're having a laugh, aren't you? Does it look like the sort of creature to be in a House of God?'

'Why not? The thing about vampires is how human they are. They could be absolutely anyone. The more human the vampire, the more attractive the story.'

'I didn't know you had theories on vampires.'

'I don't …'

'But …'

'But what?'

'You were about to say something else.'

'I was about to say something else?'

'Of course. You were about to say something else. What was it? Spit it out!'

'Nothing.'

'Come on, out with it.'

'Nothing, just that vampire stories have existed in all cultures, China, and India, for example. There's a vampire story in the *One Thousand and One Nights*. And that's before you even get started on vampire stories among the Latin American Indians. And they crop up in Judaism as well. I mean, I don't think vampires have any particular stance on religion.'

'They're not scared of crucifixes then?'

'No.'

'They don't burn if they see the sunlight or if they touch holy water?'

'No.'

'Do they have super-human strength?'

You smile.

'I guess so, yes, but you probably wouldn't realise until it was too late.'

'Well, well. And what about garlic? Does it scare them off?'

'The smell of garlic would put anyone off.'

'So you reckon they can just wander into a church?'

'Yeah, course they can. They mix with humans. That's how they survive, isn't it?'

'So how come you know so much about vampires?' she asks you. 'Do you have a brother who's an expert?'

'Yeah, his name's Google.'

She sighs, as if she's not in a hurry. She looks to one side, then turns to the front again, towards the church altar.

'Who was it?' you ask, gesturing towards the photo you can't quite make out. You're not really interested. You're just making conversation. You want to keep talking.

She watches you out of the corner of her eye and turns to stare into the distance. She takes a deep breath.

'One of the darker stories of this cursed place. A guy, just like you …'

She breaks off.

'What happened to him?' you ask her.

'He was killed, that's what.'

You look at the crowd gathered.

'Who killed him?'

'Nobody knows, that's the thing. The police have no clues to go on. Or any idea why. He had no enemies. He was shy, excelled at school, all the mums loved him, you know. But his killers destroyed him. Viciously. His body was found in a wood a few days after he went missing, blood and guts everywhere. Like some psycho film.'

She stops her story there, her face expressionless. She finally continues, 'Like they were doing it for fun, just because. No motive. Just for the sake of it. Can you imagine that?'

'And they've not caught anyone?' you ask.

She briefly shakes her head, without looking around. She squints slightly and pouts her lips.

'Whoever did it is still out there. The police are completely stumped. They say it's probably not even the first death. It's just the first one that's come to light, that's all. And now everyone's expecting a second body to appear. Or what's left of it. And meanwhile they keep holding these church services although I'm not really sure why any more. Calling for justice and all that. They do it once a month. What about you? What are you doing here? Are you visiting? Are you headed somewhere?'

'I missed my train to Madrid. Well, I didn't so much miss it; I booked the wrong day.' You smile a little shyly.

'Seriously?'

'Yeah.'

The black-eyed girl laughs, under her breath.

'What happened? Did you get confused?'

You try to look as serious as possible.

'I dunno …'

She looks at you with raised eyebrows.

'You don't know if you got it wrong?'

'People say casual mistakes don't exist.'

She nods and looks forwards again.

'Ah okay, so maybe it wasn't a mistake, maybe that's what you really wanted to do right from the start. We think we're making mistakes, but unconsciously we're actually just doing what we really want. Am I right?'

'Something like that.'

She thinks for a moment. Then she says, 'So, following your theory, if there are never any casual mistakes, if we end up doing what we truly wanted to do from the start, we never actually make any real mistakes.'

'If you're clear in your mind about what you really want. And what's good for you.'

'Why?'

'Well, sometimes you might want something but it's not good for you. Doesn't matter what it is, you're wrong to want it.'

She laughs. You want to think it's because she's impressed, but you suspect it might not be. For all you're trying to be so deep and meaningful, it doesn't seem to be working. She doesn't believe you, but she's trying to make you think she does.

'So?' she goes on.

'What?'

'Are you one of those people who wants things that are bad for them?'

You speak without thinking. If you keep talking, she might just stay with you.

'How do I know? How do you know if something's good for you or not? Loving someone who no longer feels the same way, for example. It could be good because it forces you to fight for them. But it could be bad, too, because it can just leave you all messed up.'

She smiles again.

'When do you leave? Are you staying until tomorrow?'

'Until midnight tonight. I changed my ticket to the midnight train to Madrid.'

'But you're clearly not spending the whole night here. Can't we just say that in this case, booking the wrong date was simply an honest mistake?' she asks, smiling.

You laugh before replying.

'I suppose so.'

'Can't we just say you're here by mistake and that's it?'

'Yes, we could.'

The service or whatever it was they were doing at the front finishes. You're almost sad. It feels good there, you're enjoying talking nonsense with this girl. But the people are starting to stand up, like when the film's finished and everyone has to leave the movie theatre. You feel unexpectedly lonely.

But yes, it's definitely finished. People stand around, saying goodbye, chatting in low voices, moving towards the exit with stony faces, difficult to read. And the only thing you can think of to do is stay where you are. You feel like an imposter, a gatecrasher who's just been discovered. So you don't move. And unexpectedly, your companion doesn't move either. She stays with you.

The line continues down the central aisle, shuffling towards the cold and the wind. Some of them don't even look at you. Others glance curiously in your direction. You respond by staring at the seat back in front of you, avoiding eye contact. You snuggle down into your scarf, concealing your face. In fact, you're still wearing your hat; hiding is easy.

You're good at passing unnoticed. At going unrecognised. And that's how you end up alone in the church with her. Your main emotion is relief.

'They say you ought to let the dead rest in peace,' she whispers. 'But they don't leave the living alone.'

'Do you know all these people?'

'I'm not exactly a churchy sort of girl, if that's what you're asking.'

'And you're not a fan of pink either.'

'Or dogs. Go figure.' She smiles. 'I expect I'll never make any new friends or live very long.'

'I guess not,' you say, smiling back.

'So, what from here until midnight?'

'What do you mean, "what"?'

'What are your plans?'

'I have no idea.'

She studies you for a few moments.

'Seriously, where have you come from?'

'My mom's house, in Bordeaux. I spent New Year with her.'

'Your mum lives in Bordeaux?'

'Yep. She came here after she split up with my dad.'

'And she left you in Uruguay?'

'Yeah.'

'Wow!'

'If a father does that, nobody thinks anything of it, but if a mother does it, everyone's surprised.'

'You're right, it's true. A woman has the same right to be free.'

'It's funny, if a man goes off to live with another woman in a different continent and forgets about his child, it's a typical man thing to do. 'Cos men do bastardy things like that. But if it's a woman, it's because they want to be free.'

'I meant that they both have a right to be free. But, hey, don't get started with all your theories again, all right? Just tell me what happened.'

'There's not much to tell. She fell in love with another guy and left for France. She calls me on my birthday. End of.'

'Has she had other kids?'

'Twin girls.'

'How old?'

'Seven. Beautiful. Amélie and Lucienne.'

'*Oh lá lá, vive la France.* This your first time here?'

'Second.'

'In how many years?'

'Ten.'

'You've seen your mum twice in ten years?'

'Yep.'

'So how come you're headed to Madrid?'

'This time my dad's made the most of it to visit a friend there, so I'm on my way to meet him. He wants us to do the tourist thing together.'

'You don't seem all that keen.'

'Not really.'

'So why travel by train and not plane? You scared of flying?'

'No. I fancied coming by train, that's all. I wanted to see the landscape. And my mom thought it'd be more ecological. She worries about the environment.'

'Train instead of plane, one day not the other. Sounds kind of like you wanted, I dunno, to get lost.'

'I'm not convinced that sightseeing with my dad is really what I had planned for the summer.'

'Summer? Oh yeah, it's summer in Uruguay right now, isn't it?'

You're suddenly aware of how far away you are from the summer, how far you are from Lucrecia too, from her blue eyes, from her lips on yours. Everything is opposite: summer and winter; Lucrecia and this girl; you thinking in double; and remembering *The Prince and the Pauper*.

The girl smiles and you look at her, letting yourself float away in the nocturnal sea of her gaze. You prepare to speak but realise you have nothing to say. You distract yourself for a moment with her angelic face. It's oval with strong features, a wide mouth, sensual in an unusual way. The whole montage together creates an unpredictable picture, like an accidental portrait where you focus on one thing and then something else bombs into the photo, becoming the real focus. Just like William in *Almost Famous*, you think she could be your Penny Lane, a dark-haired Penny Lane. Why not?

'Sorry …'

'Why, what's wrong?'

'Can I take a photo?'

'A photo? Of me? What for?'

She's uneasy. Photos often make people uncomfortable.

'I like taking photos. It's a sort of hobby.'

She looks at you, chewing her lower lip. And it's at that moment that she bursts out laughing. Out of nowhere. An explosion of unwonted happiness, provoked by absolutely nothing. And yet it's contagious and you can do nothing to prevent yourself from joining in, the two of you laughing at God knows what (or at least, you have no idea). It seems ridiculous, completely ridiculous, but amazing for that very same reason. It's the best thing that's happened to you since you arrived in Europe. Or since Lucrecia spoke those final seven letters.

'Sorry, sorry,' she says. 'I wasn't laughing at you.'

'I don't know what I'm laughing about either.'

'Perhaps you're laughing at me,' she remarks.

'No, no. Sometimes I just laugh for no good reason.'

She nods. You sigh.

'No, you can't take my photo. I don't like it.'

'That's fine.'

'So, what are you going to do now?' she asks.

'I told you, I don't know. Wander around.'

'Wander around? Where?'

'I dunno, around.'

41

She smiles again. You find yourself looking at her teeth as if they were something you'd never seen before.

'Are you stupid or what?'

'What do you mean? I've nothing else to do.'

She looks at you, an infinite, mysterious look, an intergalactic look. And you have the strange sensation of being carried away by it, blown along, like a leaf in the wind.

She seems amused. And curious. And there's something else, but you're not sure what. An infinite and mysterious look, that makes you feel mysterious and infinite, but you don't know why.

'You really have nothing else to do?' she asks, echoing your previous words.

'No.'

'So you're just going to roam around here?'

'Erm, yes.'

'We're in the middle of winter. And didn't you hear what I told you before? There's some psychopath out there. You're crazy, tío.'

Her accent, it kills you. Being around other people that speak like you, you forget that an accent is like music.

'Fine,' she says, anticipating your next response. 'I'll come with you. I don't want you to get lost.'

'Really?' You grin.

She widens her eyes.

'Yeah. We don't want anything to happen to you. It wouldn't be good for tourism.'

You grin again.

'Well, what could be more important than looking after this city's tourism?' I say.

That was probably one of the silliest comments in the whole history of silly comments, but she gives nothing away to suggest she found it weird.

And this is how you find yourself walking alongside her, down the central aisle of the church. It's strange, you suddenly get the taste on your tongue of the chocolate-covered raisins you ate earlier, just a hint on your palate, between your teeth, and ugh, you're so hungry, an ancestral hunger you don't know how to manage.

It's dark outside. The streetlights are all lit, orange balls floating in the violet city. There's nobody left from the gathering at the church. It must have been raining, but you didn't notice.

5

You walk a while with her, making small talk. You ask things you've never considered asking anyone before, things you think make you sound more adult: questions about life in Irun, this place you've never heard of before. And off you go, trying to show her you're interested. But the whole time, you feel like an imposter. Because you're only interested in her, not what she's telling you.

You're not sure how to change the topic without making it look like everything you've talked about so far has been completely unnecessary, false. And you wonder, too, how much you ought to try and find out about her. Maybe this girl doesn't want to tell you anything about herself and she's comfortable as she is. What sort of questions aren't too intrusive? Footsteps pass, minutes, while the cold penetrates your clothing and freezes your scalp, despite your hat. The pain in your head lets up a little, although the temperature doesn't help. In any case, you're enjoying the walk. And the company.

Until the silence arrives. You can barely hear the soles of your feet or hers on the wet concrete. And that's when you ask it. You don't know where the question comes from. You just say it. No forward planning.

'So, did you know the … the kid well?'

You don't dare say the word *dead* and you feel a weakness, but you can't do anything about it because your hesitation is part of the world you share with this girl.

'Who?'

'The one from the church. I mean, was he your friend or something?'

The photo had been off to one side, so you never really had a good look. And you presume that's why she'd entered the church, although you can't be sure. You hope the question hasn't upset her; you're already regretting having asked it.

'Oh,' she says, her eyes forward, as if she's having a quick conversation with herself. 'Have you ever known anyone who died?'

'Erm, no, not really.'

'Not even your grandparents?'

'Well, yeah, them. My grandma on my mom's side died just before my mom came to France. The other one on my dad's side died a few years back. I didn't really know my grandads.'

'So they died when you were very little?'

'One died before I was even born. The other passed away when I was one.'

'That's a shame.'

'Yeah.'

'Really, I'm sorry.'

'I would have liked to have known them,' you remark. 'Even just one of them. I don't remember the one who died when I was one.'

'No, of course not.'

She seems buried deep in thoughts you can't make out from the surface. You wonder if you ought to change the subject again, but you get the feeling you'll get it wrong whatever you say. She speaks next.

'I know it's awful when a grandparent dies, but just imagine if it's one of your friends.'

Suddenly, you feel out of place. This journey through Irun, the walk with the girl, it's all somehow out of place. You have no idea what to say.

'Yeah ... I'm sorry.'

'It's so ... unnatural.'

You stay silent. She's still submerged in something you can't work out, and you don't know how to confront it. You conclude that the best thing to do is wait. You're learning to be patient. Waiting is a weapon.

'D'you fancy a surprise?' she asks.

'What?'

'I said, do you fancy a surprise?'

You don't know. Nobody's ever asked you that before. That's kind of the whole point, isn't it? They don't ask first.

'Maybe you don't like surprises?' she insists.

'Er, yeah, I guess I do.'

'Well, here goes: my friend looked exactly like you.'

'Wha—?'

'How do you like that as a surprise, hey? Identical. You're like twins.'

'What d'you—'

This second interjection sounds more emphatic than the previous one, but the girl has managed to surprise you, so much so that you're incapable of finishing a whole sentence. You try all the same.

'I don't understand.'

'Identical. I almost didn't believe it myself when I saw you in the plaza. That's why I came over to talk to you, to reassure myself that I wasn't going crazy. I wanted to confirm that despite the fact you're hiding behind your scarf and hat, you really are identical.'

'How can we be identical?'

'I swear to you. You're like a living ghost in flesh and bone.'

'There's no way we can be identical.'

'I don't have a phone otherwise I'd show you a photo and you'd see. No doubt about it! And I don't just mean a little bit alike. I mean, like properly identical, tío.'

47

There's something in all of this that makes you uneasy and yet you're fascinated by the suggestion.

'There's no way that can be true. I mean, how would that even work?'

You've gone and ruined it all again with your habit of talking too much. Will you ever learn? But the girl goes on serenely.

'If you saw him now, you'd say, "What am I doing in another person's body? That's impossible!" But of course, you can't. Because he's dead.'

You can't tell if she said that to be funny. The idea of a body, the spitting image of yours, dying, it's like something from another universe. One part of you considers leaving now and going to look at that photo in the church, but at this time of night, it's probably closed. The other part of you really doesn't fancy seeing your double who died. You're not sure you could bear it. Although it would mean no longer being the pauper and becoming the prince, that much is true. Someone alive is always the prince compared with someone who's not there. But you know that's an absurd thing to think, so you stop. You don't feel like the prince of anything.

And you really don't want to give this girl the impression you don't trust her, that you don't believe what she's telling you. You want her to stay with you to the end.

'Whenever a young person dies it's horrific,' she sighs. 'But when you think about how he died ... it's so much worse.'

48

A strange terror washes over you, a ridiculous terror, too, because you're alive. But for some reason your mind bombards you with images suggesting it was you who died, that with the whole Lucrecia thing, somehow, you did *actually* die.

And you complete the story in your head. You imagine that by walking into that church, you were attending your own funeral, and that you're now nothing more than a tormented soul, roaming around a lost city. Where does your brain get these things from? You try to turn it off, like a TV, but you can't.

At first you thought it'd be difficult, dramatic even, for Penny Lane to talk about all this. But she does it so calmly, remaining emotionless, for the most part. The story unfolds easily, as if she is in no way involved. She speaks again, her eyes still forward, as if to say something as we walk.

'They say there are seven people in the world who look like us. I'm not sure if it's true.'

'Seven? Can't be.'

'Well, I'm not sure about seven, but there must be doubles out there. In fact, there was some photographer guy who dedicated his life to just that.'

'To what?'

'Looking for doubles. He travelled around the world photographing them. I don't mean siblings, but people who were identical but had never met. They didn't even know each other existed. Look it up on the internet. It's bizarre, I tell you.'

Suddenly you want to leave, escape this conversation, Irun, these eight hours. And you wonder how to do it without leaving any evidence. But it's obvious you're not actually going to do it. Your fate — or at least your fate as far as the midnight train — is tied to this girl. You want to find out about her. You want to kiss her. Something so simple and yet so radical as pressing your lips against her slender, graceful neck, and staying there, kissing her for all eternity as she closes her eyes. Your senses long to expand, to unfurl like tentacles into the world, towards her. It's a senseless image but your head hasn't stopped spinning since you met her in the square.

When your mind comes back to the present, you're both walking. You have no idea where to or why, but you don't care. Before, you didn't know your final destination; now you prefer not to. May the devil take care of the details. You don't want to know where this girl is leading you. But if it means she's leading you somewhere, you just want her to take you there. You're in a weird road movie, walking, but you can't — and you don't want to — get out. And she finally does what you've been hoping she'll do for a while now: she interrupts your thoughts.

'You okay?' she asks you.

'Yeah, course.'

'It's just, your face …'

You look at her, holding your breath a moment. What's wrong with your face? She doesn't say specifically, that's all she says. You imagine it's pale, or excessively red, the colour it usually turns at the worst possible moments, and there's never anything you can do about it.

'Well …' she goes on, 'you see, the thing is, I was thinking about the boy's grandpa. The boy who was killed, I mean.'

She's looking forward again, as if this helps to steady her emotions.

'What's wrong with his grandpa?'

You feel it's your duty to continue the conversation.

'He's fine. He just forgets things. He's got … what's it called? He mixes people up, he forgets what he's just said. Sometimes he has absolutely no idea what on earth he's doing. I mean, as I say, he's fine, really. Not like perfect-perfect. D'you get what I mean? But anyway. The only complicated thing, the only thing that's complicated, is his memory.'

'Oh.'

'They've tried several times to explain to him what's happened. To his grandson, I mean. The two were really close, you know? Inseparable. But it's no use. He forgets everything. And then they have to explain it all over again. Going over all those details. Telling him what's happened. Can you imagine? Re-telling the same thing over and over. Repeating that terrible death again and again.'

She speaks as if all this was normal. As if it's some everyday problem. Nothing about her suggests she's discussing anything more than the weather, or so it seems.

51

You find her hard to read. She makes you curious. All you want to do is continue watching her, listening to her. And it's not as if she's even doing anything special to get your attention. It's just happening, that's all. Something you can't, and don't want to prevent.

'So, anyway,' she continues, as you keep walking along the roads you don't recognise. (Where are you exactly? Could you find your way back to the station? Whatever. You're sure you'd find someone to ask the way, and there's still plenty of time. You're not exactly sure what time it is, but you're sure there's still time.) 'We make up stories. "Oh, he's gone away." "He'll be back soon." "Ah, he's at work at the moment." "He's out with his girlfriend, with his friends ..." Anything so we don't have to tell him the real story again. Not with that ending.'

'You know him, then? The grandpa?'

'Well, yeah.'

And what if all this is just lies. Perhaps the only thing this girl's doing is playing with you. A pathological liar who's mocking you. Or maybe it's not so innocent. At the end of the day, who is she?

You have no idea. But what are you going to do? Resist now? You didn't want to do that before, less still now. You don't want to resist; you want to be with her, with your Penny Lane. You want to find out everything about her, and yet all she does is keep talking in this same way, so ... you can't find the right word for it. How is she speaking? As if she's known you for ages, which does nothing other than increase your feeling that maybe it's all true. Perhaps your double really did exist out there. And she knew him. A lie like that is too absurd. The only alternative is that it must be the truth.

Mouthfuls of cold air open up tiny slits in your lungs. And from out of nowhere, you know exactly what the girl's going to say next, what she's going to suggest. You know how this conversation will end. You know where she's going with it. You know why she's come up with this story of the double.

It's a ridiculous proposal and you can't believe she's actually going to say it, but you're sure that's where she's headed. You watch her with a sharpness you're not used to. And yet, you can't blame her that it's all ended up like this. Ultimately, it occurred to you, too.

'I thought you could go and visit him,' she says simply.

You have to pretend to be surprised, like a pantomime. The pantomime is that of course it's impossible, it's ridiculous. If you're honest, it's not a pretence. It really is ridiculous.

'Visit who?'

She looks sideways at you and smiles again, one of her smiles that's difficult to interpret. She avoids the question, although it's obvious: *Who do you think?* But she leaves it unspoken. Instead, she says, 'I know it's not fair to ask, and I don't even know you, but you're leaving at midnight and there won't be another chance like this.'

'Chance for what?' you insist. You need to hear it. You need to hear her say it.

'So he can be with his grandson, of course.'

'But I'm not his grandson!' you exclaim, without too much emphasis. 'He'll notice.'

'Of course he won't.'

'And even if he does believe it, even if he is confused, what would the point be? He'll forget it anyway.'

'His brain, of course, would forget. But I think a part of him would remember, you know? Don't ask me what or how, but it would save the memory. In his heart or something, I dunno. Something like that. It's not a lot, I know, but it's something, at least. A moment of happiness. And perhaps it sounds like nonsense, but—'

'He's not my grandpa.'

'No, of course he isn't. And I get it completely if you say no. Hey, look, forget it. Just pretend I said nothing. It's an absurd idea.'

More than absurd, it's unfair. Of course it's unfair, you think. It's beastly. It's monstrous. How could someone ask you to do that? Especially someone you don't know.

'It'd never end well.'

'Why not?'

'Because it wouldn't. It could never end well.'

But then again … then again, you imagine playing the part of having a grandpa. For the first time.

'So what if it goes wrong?' she continues. 'You're leaving at midnight in any case, and from then on, it'd be like nothing had ever happened, like none of this had ever existed. At the very least, it's something to do until you have to leave. I know you don't know me. You probably think I'm sick in the head or something. That's what other people say.'

You feel like you've slipped into something familiar, like the first time you ride a bike again after not touching it for a while. You climb on and you stay there, even when you think you've forgotten how. The first cold impression of the metal object, before your body and the bike mould together, until one is the extremity of the other. Reflexes, balance and instinct become one.

'He'll notice,' you insist.

'Even if he thinks something's a bit weird, I reckon his brain will instantly accept the lie. He'll want to. Don't ask me why, but if I'm sure of something, it's that. The more I talk to you, the more similar you are.'

'They'll spot my accent.'

'Well, act then.'

'What do you mean, act? I don't do acting.'

'We're acting the whole time. Our lives are one great parody.'

'Don't start with all that …'

But it's true. Of course you're acting your whole life. You've just spent three weeks acting in your mother's house.

Trying to be fine with it all, making out you're enjoying it, as if you're happy to be there when in reality, you couldn't wait to leave. Even now, you've been pretending to be surprised, just a few short minutes ago, when you weren't even trying. You're a consummate actor.

The two of you walk a little further and the ground feels like it's turned to sludge, catching your feet and not letting you go. Like your boyish nightmares where you're trying to escape some monster that's chasing you, especially the nightmares after your mother left. Always thinking it would have been good to have a brother. Or a sister. Not like your French sisters, who are barely even acquaintances, but someone for you to share what was happening with. And it would have been good to have a grandpa, even just for a while. Because your family is so small. So small and so divided.

'I'd love to explain how it feels to see you again,' she says. 'To talk to you. I know it's the first time I've seen you, it's not that. I just get the feeling … It's fine. I get if you don't want to do it. In your place, I definitely wouldn't. It's just that it seems like it's for such a good reason. But I'm used to people looking at me weirdly when I say what I think. I told you about that before.'

And you know the dice have been thrown. That this meandering walk has brought you to this moment from which there is no return. You will end up going. Even if you don't want to do it. And you don't want to. But you also don't want to leave this girl walking beside you. In fact, if it had been anyone else, would you have even gone this far? Of course not.

But it's her. You want to please her. You want to see her smile. Without worrying too much about why. You know you should be thinking about the family, but the truth is, you just don't care. Her story about the grandpa sounds great to you, it's all so well thought out. And so you keep walking in silence.

'It's not too far, but it's not close either,' she comments.

'What is?'

'The house where my friend's grandpa lives.'

'Oh.'

'I'll take you there. But we can't put it off, you know what I mean? Put off making a decision, I mean.'

And this is how you close your eyes, for a second, enjoying the feeling of being led, thinking that you know how all of this is going to end, although you're still not entirely sure you know how you want it to end.

After all, what is it you want?

6

You're won over by the certainty that there's a tacit agreement between you and Penny Lane, a collusion that requires no words. Meanwhile, you just keep walking. You feel shadows around you again, shadows lying in wait. Irun has become indecipherable in the last few minutes, as the night closes in above your head. You pass a globe of light as you walk beneath one of the streetlamps and it's impossible for you to say exactly where you're headed. You play down the importance of knowing. It's a cold, cloudy night, but to a certain point, it's peaceful. To be honest, despite how bizarre all of this is, you're happy to be living in the moment. You're enjoying every second. This is just what you needed.

You have no concept of when the city of Irun becomes less built-up and more wooded. If you wanted to escape, it's too late now. You're going to need the girl's help to get back to the station. Or maybe you won't. You're sure you'd find a way. But that's not the point. What you do know is that each step you take — like it or not — draws you further and further into an urban legend. You're wandering through a deserted place with a girl you know nothing about. You've agreed where to go with her, but you have no idea how to get there. Or back. You think you know who she is, but in all honesty, you don't have a clue. You should probably distance yourself from her, but all you do is keep getting closer.

You remember all the times you were told not to trust strangers: don't go with them, don't follow them, and *never* tell *anyone* your name. And yet, here you are, disobeying all the warnings. Warnings, warnings, warnings. Telling you to walk away, to turn around and break away from this girl you know nothing about. But you don't want to. Of course you don't. That's why you're here, ignoring the orders that reach you from somewhere in the past. This is it, you tell yourself. At some point you have to stop doing what they all tell you to do.

'We're nearly there,' the girl says, and you look up and down the street you're on. It's a path crossing a desolate part of the city. There are a few trees dotted among the bushes.

The path leads towards a house standing on a hill. Its angular shape cuts into the ground, like something straight out of *Psycho*. One shadow on top of another, only that the clouds are ashen, so all you can make out is the black shape of the building.

It's the quietest place in the world. Or so it seems. All you can hear is the wind. And your own breathing. The wind of your breathing.

And you're off, you're going there. Revisiting a memory. You know what it is, all too well. Or rather who. Even though you don't want to.

'What are you thinking about?' she asks you.

'Nothing.'

'Come on, tío. I can hear the cogs in your brain turning from here.'

In your mind you see the piece of paper that Lucrecia gave you. There are the verses written in her careful, rounded letters.

'I was remembering a poem.'

'Oh really?! Please don't come at me now with poetry readings and all that, because—'

'No, I don't read poetry. All I said was that I was remembering a poem.'

'What poem?'

'One I was given as a present. It's not important.'

You walk a little further. The moon walks across the sky with you before disappearing behind a cloud.

'Aren't you scared?' she asks.

'Of what?'

'Being here, in this place.'

'Why? Should I be scared?'

'I don't know. What do you reckon?'

You take a deep breath. You control a tremor of nerves within.

'I'm not easily frightened.'

She smiles.

'Is that because you read so many horror books?'

'*Dracula*'s not a horror story! Really, all vampire tales are just kind of love stories, that's all.'

'Seriously? Whatever!'

You speak to silence the voice in your head, to distract yourself from other thoughts. Because you have to wait. You know you have to wait. You're learning.

'Yeah!'

She laughs.

'Yeah, yeah. But anyway, I'm still surprised you came with me.'

'How come?'

'I mean, it's obvious, isn't it? I'm such a *good* girl and all that.'

It's clear something is wrong. Something is out of place. Every cell of your body is screaming at you, but you still feel incapable of resisting her. You like her too much. And even if you wanted to control yourself, you can't. So why bother.

Something moves nearby. You're not sure what it is. Perhaps it's the wind blowing the branches. But something is about to happen; you don't need super extra-sensory powers to guess that much. And anyway, it's not like you can avoid it now; you agreed to throw the dice. Nothing's changed. You think about Lucrecia again. Lucrecia. Always Lucrecia.

It must be because the girl's just been asking you about vampire stories, but you're happy not to know her name. And you're still thrilled to be with her. You want this night to last for ever. Even if it's just the once.

'But,' she whispers, 'the truth is, you don't know me. You don't know anything about me. Not even my name.'

You clear your throat.

'That's true.'

'And you have no way of knowing if my story is real.'

'What story?'

'The one about my friend, your double. You have no way of knowing if there really is someone else identical to you.'

You lick your lips and take a deep breath.

'Of course there is. Didn't you say there's seven of me somewhere?'

'That's just a myth. Something someone just said. How can they really know? I mean, the thing about the photos of identical doubles is true, but still. It's all a question of believing.'

You don't respond immediately. But neither do you slow your pace. Something within you doesn't want to break the rhythm, this melody. You're in the middle of a dance.

'Maybe.'

'Maybe you don't actually have a double.'

'Maybe I don't.'

'Maybe there's no grandpa waiting for his dead grandson.'

'Maybe not.'

'Maybe you can't play at being a ghost in flesh and bones today. Maybe you can't play at being, you know, the living dead.'

The girl lets out a peal of laughter that falls through the sky like petals. She's happy and you can't help feeling the same. And although there is some perversion in this happiness, you can't refuse to share this feeling with her. Even the cold feels pleasant. Your mouth waters more than usual and you realise that this is why, this very moment is why you opted to take the train. For the adventure. For a detour. And perhaps that's why you messed up the tickets. There are no such things as casual errors. Or are there?

'Maybe you're right and I can't play at being anything,' you concur.

She finally steps in front of you, stops and looks at you, still with that smile and sweetness. You can't wait any longer to kiss her. Perhaps this is it. You never know if it's the right moment. You've not done it enough to feel certain.

You flare your nostrils. You want to catch her scent.

'D'you fancy a surprise?' she asks you again.

You close your eyes, and you sense the movement behind you, even before it happens.

Never mind.

The blow to your head is brutal, enough to break your skull, and the pain that follows — and of course it does follow — is as black as the night itself, like the shadow of that house silhouetted against the cloudy sky. It's a black sea that blinds you, causing you to fall into a bottomless tank. It's a petrol tank drowning you with a spark that turns to fire. It's an unforgettable moment. One you'll never forget, even if you want to.

Whoever hit you takes advantage of the moment to attack you on the ground. You're sure they're kicking you, but it feels distant. Something that's causing your body to jerk, forcing the breath from your lungs, creating an internal turmoil, bursting your tiny blood vessels. It hurts, of course it does, but it's nothing compared to the pain in your head. And that's what gives the impression of distance. They shake you and pull you around. Their hands are anxious. You can smell the adrenalin surging like a river through their veins.

You're dizzy and on the ground so you don't register where they are, but the faces of the girl and a boy you've not seen before now loom into view. But hold on, haven't you seen him before? Didn't you meet him in Irun? Did you see him and not register his face? Like a video on rewind, you go back over each step you've taken this evening. You see the city again. You take another step back. Maybe you did see him, or maybe not, but yes. His image comes back to you, bumping into you accidentally at the exit to the train station, apologising with a gesture, with his John Lennon glasses, continuing on past.

And now they're both there — the girl and the boy — deformed because you can't focus properly, silhouetted against a sky daubed with charcoal. The girl looks at you then turns to the recent arrival. Finally, her black eyes rest back on you.

'Ahh, now I see it. You don't look as much like my friend as I thought.' She grins.

You could give them the camera. Tell them to take it, but they're not interested in that. Nobody's interested in your freaking 500-euro camera. You could offer them a chest-full of diamonds and they still wouldn't be interested. The last thing they want is something material. This isn't a robbery; it's something else. Another game, another sport, another galaxy. It's not about the money. This is about pleasure. This is about some repressed desire breaking through. This is another dimension.

Another image floats above your head. It's her, telling you about the murder: *Whoever did it is still free.*

Free.

They drag you across the grass and you understand why you felt them pulling your body about in between the blows: they've bound your legs together and strapped your wrists behind your back with thick grey sticky tape. They've not actually tied you up very well, not really, but they don't care; it's effective. For now, at least.

That's why they're dragging you. You let them do it. You don't speak, you don't break the silence. In the confusion of the moment, with this strange distance you're experiencing, it doesn't occur to you to stop them. They drag you on and on, without glancing back. As they heave you across the ground, all you can think about is how they're damaging your clothes. They're new. Your mother bought them for you in Bordeaux.

The girl's holding onto one side, the boy onto the other. You decide to watch him. Red hair, freckles. Older than you. Perhaps older than her, too. The first thing you think is that he looks like such a nice boy, an advanced student of philosophy, perhaps. You're not sure what makes you think he might be intellectual. Could it be the glasses? He's got long curly hair that covers and expands his head. His skin is pale and his face looks kind. While he appears quite young, you notice there's a look in his eyes which suggests a mournful aging.

And on top of all that, you recognise his hunger. You see it in his eyes, in his movements, in everything about him. A type of hunger that will never be satiated by anything. A hunger much worse than your own.

They pull you into the vegetation, in a direction you can't figure out. You'd prefer to be unconscious, but your consciousness remains firmly in place, fixed to your brain until the end. At some point, they cover your mouth with the same tape. It's annoying and the taste which slips in

66

through a tiny gap between your lips is revolting. You hate having it there; it's as if it goes all the way down your throat.

'I told you,' she says. 'I told you it'd be easy.'

The boy doesn't respond, he's busy moving you. He's the one who takes most of the weight, your weight. Between them flows a dialogue of hunters, as much for the way they speak as the words themselves. No. There are many different types of hunters, you tell yourself. The Weimaraner from before springs to mind, its face almost smiling. A good dog.

A pale, incomplete moon appears in the dark vault above you. You never could grasp the whole waxing or waning thing. However much you try, you just don't get it. The wind is cold and bitter, it smells of earth and rocks. A swelling grows on your neck, like a balloon, inflating and deflating between the bone and the skin.

You try to relax and wait. As they carry you, they bump you around. But finally, they're satisfied. They seem to have reached some planned spot, or perhaps it's just that this place will do. Remote and isolated. They throw you to the ground and you feel twigs digging into your back, the hard irregularity of the earth. It's spongy, but firm.

You're there, face up, gasping at air through your nose, waiting. They grab hold of you, one on each side. Their heads are spheres, bubbles, planets that appear before your eyes. He pushes his glasses up his nose and grins. His teeth are even but really rather small. And as his upper lip pulls back, you can see a lot of his gumline. There's something babyish in his smile, but without the freshness. Everything about him is dry, completely dry. Whatever he hit you with is just out of view, or at least, you can't see it.

'Great.' You hear him speak for the first time. He has a soft, cultivated voice, melodic. 'Let's have some fun!'

She smiles and takes her phone out of her pocket, the phone she said she didn't have. She points it towards you, preparing to take a photo, until she spots your camera. She smiles again. She removes it carefully, hanging it elegantly around her own neck, with an air somewhere between naughty and professional. She turns it on and photographs you, taking her time to focus properly. Over and over.

You've already put the pieces together in your head. Like a trail in the forest. Blood and guts everywhere. Like some psycho film. Despite the darkness, you notice a gleam in the pair's eyes. It's the thrill of the hunt. You recognise it easily. For them, you're nothing more than meat. But not to eat, of course. Not to feed some bodily hunger like yours, but a mental hunger. You feel sorry for them. A hunger like that can't ever be stilled.

Just for the fun of it. Can you imagine?

She giggles. It was just as Penny Lane had told you: those who killed the boy in the church, your supposed double, were lying in wait. Of course they were. Ironically, during your few short hours in Irun you've discovered more than the police have in months. You found them!

68

And yet, while Penny Lane and the redhead may be different to you, and have nothing at all to do with you, you find you understand them perfectly.

You understand the hunt, although the reasons behind it are different. Prey is always the promised land. In the same way, you completely understand that if you're going to hunt someone, it's better to choose someone unknown. Someone like you. That way, nobody's going to link you to it. The victim has to be random. And better still if it's someone on a journey. More time before they find the body. If they ever do. It's all very logical.

You finish that thought and observe them carefully, their necks and throats. Their throats in particular. In his case, you can see his swollen jugular. In hers, you can make out the beating, encased in a delicate layer of skin. A furious ocean flows beneath, quicker now that they've caught you. *I've crossed oceans of time to find you.* Isn't that what Bram Stoker wrote?

He stops giggling, but the last trail of it takes on an unpleasant tone, like a puppy coughing. His face turns ratty, although you're not entirely sure why.

The redhead rummages through his backpack for something. He's pleased you're awake and for some reason you wonder why you didn't fight harder for Lucrecia. Why did you accept that she was finishing with you, no questions asked? You're not used to fighting, that's why. Why is it you're not used to fighting?

'Are you scared?' he asks you, ripping the tape off your lips.

'No,' you reply, and for a second, you see the look in his eyes. More than surprise, there's displeasure. He wants you to be frightened. Saying no is like taking away a sweetie from a small child. Is that what makes him hungry? Your fear? Is he hungry for fear?

Why don't you fight?

You really want a greater surprise, but it's not going to happen. Not today. You've decided that now is fine. It's time for everyone else to get used to the fact that you *do* fight. Up to now you've been the pauper. But you're about to become the prince.

7

With one jerk of your arms, the tape stretches enough for you to move your hands and tear it off. You've liberated yourself. You're free. It's taken just the blink of an eye, from one second to the next. And now you see the faces of the other two, frozen.

They weren't expecting that. And less still for it to happen so quickly, so easily. And it's more than the fact that the tape wasn't tight enough. They didn't see your strength. This strength doesn't belong to a mere sixteen-year-old boy. It's a strength that goes way beyond the norm, and they have no idea. Not yet. It's not their fault, but it is their crime, their mortal defect. They didn't see it and therein lies their ruin. You're unsure of your own limits — only now are you starting to understand them — but you do know it's a strength that cannot be restrained by sticky tape, and that's enough for now.

They're still not alarmed; they're in serial-killer mode. They can't get over their astonishment. It's difficult for them

71

to shift from one feeling to the other and their transitions are slow. And they've not yet realised that this is where it all ends.

Your movements, like lightning, are completely off-script. Chances are they had a carefully written plan in their heads of how this was all going to play out and what they would do with you. You escaping was not part of the movie.

Even now as the redhead sees you raise your arms and lift your body a little way off the ground, there's something clouding his vision. You think it's fear, but truthfully, you have no idea. Maybe, you think, maybe it's incomprehension more than anything. Or incredulity. His internal landscape — his real self — is concealed from you. It makes you curious, but only a little. You imagine it to be dry and desert-like. Grey, cracked earth. But anyhow, whatever the redhead might be thinking, whatever feelings might be residing within his heart and soul, they are his last ones. There won't be any more.

You stretch out your two hands, grip his skull and jerk it sharply, like a whip. His neck snaps and it's game over for the redhead. He falls, motionless, and Penny Lane — your black-eyed Penny Lane, the same one that hooked you in with so many captivating words, the same one that just seconds earlier had photographed you for all eternity — tries to scream. Her jugular swells as she opens her mouth and attempts to flee. She desperately staggers backwards, your camera bouncing around her neck.

It's foolish on her part. You've already forced your legs apart, ripped the tape off with your hands and clambered to your feet. You make a gesture using the palm of your right hand, entreating her to calm down, but she carries on as before, exercising her vocal cords to the max. It doesn't matter, though; it's only a scream. It was she who brought you here where nobody can hear you. You'd like to point out the irony of the situation, but something tells you she might not see it. Even so, her wide-open mouth displays all her teeth, and you think about the teeth, the teeth, the teeth.

Her instinct is to flee, but she can't. She's just shuffling backwards. Her brain hasn't sent the right message to the rest of her body. You walk, keeping close. You let her scream, and you think of Lucrecia. Lucrecia, Lucrecia … You think about how to fight for her, how to forget her. Two opposing feelings in a debate, one against the other, co-habiting.

It's strange to remember her now, but then again, how could you not? This world of doubles that Penny Lane mentioned to you is well-inhabited, herself included, tied to you. You think about that, processing it all quickly. Your mind's become a whirlwind. You also think about kissing her, about how hungry you've been for so long. The same hunger that brought you here.

'Don't be scared,' you say to her in the calmest voice you can muster.

You know it's useless; she's going to be scared anyway. She's already scared. Terrified, more like. You wonder about her fear. Did she get as far with you as she had expected? You, tied up, at her mercy, abandoned in this field. Is she scared of what she was going to do to you — whatever that was going to be — because you might be about to do the same now to her? Whatever it is, you're not interested in prolonging her agony, so you lean towards her and pin her arms down next to her body.

It's easy, even though she tries to wriggle away. At some moment she must realise it's pointless, but she still tries. There's something marvellous, ingenious, and foolish in all this. You remove the camera gently. It's not much, but you know what, it was a gift from your mother. And then you embrace Penny Lane.

Her perfume blazes. She's your Penny Lane. Or is Penny Lane Lucrecia? Your head's confused, your thoughts spin, crowding your mind. You try to straighten them out. And you say whatever comes to mind.

'It's called *Una vez — Once*.'

You see her panicked expression, her bulging eyes, the terror of not having the slightest idea what you are talking about. There's nothing more terrifying than ignorance. And nothing more liberating.

'The poem,' you say. 'The one I mentioned before. The one I was remembering.'

Her movements are restricted and she tries to turn her face away from yours. But all she achieves is to display more of her throat, leaving it more exposed.

'It's about two lovers who go out for a walk one evening,' you explain.

She still doesn't understand, and you wonder if she's believed everything you've told her up to now. Most of it was true. You really did like her, right from the moment you saw her. Despite her lies. And they were incredible lies, the purest form of art. And efficient too; they brought you this far. But it brought her here, too.

'In the poem, they take a walk,' you continue, 'and, even though there's no music, they walk to the beat. They ascend into the sky, shrouded by the stars, into the night. So much so that they become the night.'

Then finally, you kiss her, right there on the neck, on the jugular. It's a kiss with teeth, it breaks the skin. You cross a boundary, like plunging into a swimming pool, but without the initial dive. Rather you slide in until all your senses are submerged in the water. A sea sweeps into your mouth, bringing with it the taste of nerves, of expectation, that was rising up from your belly for this very moment. A dense, profuse silence explodes around you like a bomb.

It's a kiss with hints of musical melodies, golden colours, the whole world. It's a kiss with the knowledge of imagination, the memory of Lucrecia. It's a kiss that takes you back to that sunrise over the beach, the holiday when you met her. And while the sky was tinged with orange, she watched the horizon and talked of the poet Circe Maia. She astonished you by reciting the final stanza from memory and then she opened a wound on her arm and let you drink. Her hunger was contagious, and you caught it. It was the only way you could contract it: blood from a blood-drinker to become one yourself.

Since that sunrise, the orange sky had not left you. It hasn't left you, even now. A brilliant iridescence occupies the closed night and sets itself alight above your head, illuminating you, cooking you. The clouds are flames, burning tongues that cross and slither across one another like snakes. And you're down below, burning, devouring the light and in turn being devoured.

This was all to forget Lucrecia, you tell yourself. And yet you're remembering her all the same. It's contradictory, of course, but that's how it is. You're the home of opposites. The blood of someone else to forget the original blood … But in the act of drinking, you can do nothing but think of Lucrecia: the girl with heavenly eyes, denim shorts, the girl from the road movie, from a rock song.

This isn't perhaps the moment to fight for Lucrecia, but the moment to fight for yourself. Maybe it's the moment to cross a border you don't entirely recognise. Whatever it is, in this moment you're living now, as you drink, and drink, this kiss, this one now, tastes of all that.

The sky in flames.

8

You finish feeding and you break away. Your head is feeling dizzy, but it clears quickly. Your senses sharpen. You hear more; your surroundings are illuminated, even though it's still dark. You can perceive smells; through your fingertips the air is a tumultuous jumble. Your mouth is exploding with sensations. Now, the rough ground vibrates with fragrances that follow the laws of the jungle, that kill each other, that dance with one another. The breeze blows sinister and aromatic, caressing the leaves, whispering to them. All around you hear tiny footsteps receding.

You feel sick, but you're not alarmed. It might just be a head rush. You still have a lot to learn. Up to now, Lucrecia was your guide. She helped you to understand, to recognise your limits. Until now. From this point on, something new has begun. You're starting something new. That same morning, she explained everything to you. That's when she introduced you to the voice. That's how she described it to you that first time. *There's something I want you to meet;*

77

it's a voice. It's incredible to describe it like that. This new instinct. What you have become through her is much more than simply a voice. And yet, it can be summarised as such. As a voice. An internal voice. A voice that guides you, like a compass. A voice that knows before you even realise it.

The first time she let you drink, you spent the day vomiting.

'It's fine, don't worry,' she said, smiling. 'It's normal to feel a bit rough. It's normal to suffer a little. It's necessary.'

When she said that, you thought it was a bit odd, out of nowhere, as if she was trying to convey something else and would take any opportunity to tell you. You thought it was a complex message, but really, it was simple: she was pulling away from you, and you didn't even notice. And she was giving you a warning. She was getting close to you only to pull away again. While she may have been attached to your body as she said it, even then she was pulling away. She was moving away, and you were just there, completely ignorant of the fact. Because the decision had already been made: she was going to disappear from your life. Although, if you're honest, a small part of you already knew. A part that didn't want to listen. Being with Lucrecia was like opening your eyes … and then closing them again. Squeezing them tightly shut. Shutting them so you couldn't see. Shutting them so you weren't frightened. Because love, too, can be a monster.

You look at the two bodies lying in the grass. Penny Lane is still beautiful, perhaps even more so now that you stop to look at her. The delicate curl of her eyelashes. An unimaginable dimple in her chin. The shape of her jawline. How slender her fingers, the soft curve of her ankles. So much beauty brings a lump to your throat. The voice doesn't make you immune to beauty, more like exactly the opposite.

You arrange her limbs so she looks as presentable as possible, despite her paleness and the wound to her neck. You lie her on her back, looking up at the sky. You spread out her hair across the grass. You straighten her clothing. You pick up your camera. There's you, the photos she took of you. They're not bad, really quite good even. As you look at them, you smile. You flick through them at your leisure, thinking that at some point you'll have to delete them, of course, but not today. Not tonight.

And then you look at her, Penny Lane, through the lens. It's a sublime picture, dazzling, like that first image you had of her against the branches and the sky. Like the second picture too, superimposed on the angels in the church. She's so beautiful you feel sad not to snap a photo, but clearly you can't. You're not even going to try. She asked you not to photograph her and you're going to respect that. And besides, you don't want anything that might link you back to her. Just in case.

As for him, you were never interested in him. You'd prefer to just leave him as he is. Whatever happens, it'll take them a while to find the bodies. Long enough at least for you to no longer be there. There's nothing to link you to them. Even if someone saw you with the girl, it won't be easy for them to recognise you, not with your hat and scarf covering almost your whole face. But whatever they do, they'll be too late.

Midnight approaches. You feel it in the air, an internal clock you have within. A minute before, your lips were on her neck and you know that in that moment, time ran differently. In that moment as you drank, an hour became a second. A lifetime in the blink of an eye. That's why it's time to go. All you need now is to clean up properly. You were careful, of course you were. You straighten your clothes — they aren't torn after all — paying close attention to the details. You pick up your scarf, strewn on the ground. Your hat, too. You recreate your original self. And you're ready. You walk away with steps that seem to happen far from your head, all the way down there, walking on cotton wool. Your legs are strong and firm, you've stopped feeling the cold. Thank goodness. You hate the cold.

The vomiting suddenly catches you off guard. You bend over to avoid any problems, so that what needs to escape can escape. Carefully, without splashing yourself. Your body purges itself, and even if your belly now feels a bit topsy turvy, this just sharpens your senses even more. The sixth sense that will lead you back to the station finally kicks in; it's as if you've lived your whole life in Irun. What was before a mass of confusion is now simple, like following a trail of breadcrumbs. It all feels so familiar.

You've still got a few minutes. You're not in a hurry, there's no need to run. You decide to take a longer route, to make the most of the invigorating night air. Out of nowhere, you start humming the song that Lucrecia always seemed to dedicate to you: *'Seguir viviendo sin tu amor'* — 'Continue Living Without Your Love' — the version by Catupecu. An old song with new DNA. Like you, this song is just another double. You search for it on your phone and connect your earphones. Soon, the chords on the violin play in your ears.

Just as the audio played in your ears the night it all started. The memory floods back like a flaming postcard. It's a warm summer's night, you're outside at a house party. You're roaming around on your own near the swimming pool where more than one person is swimming. It's a party where you barely know anyone. It's a second of solitude and bewilderment. But it's also a moment where you step away from the mass and unexpectedly hear the song. Out of nowhere. Surrounding you.

Seguir viviendo sin tu amor.

It's coming from inside. Hearing it is like finding someone you know. You leave the laughter of the pool and step inside, staggering slightly, following the music.

You think the lyrics are saying that you can choose the person you love. You often feel — although you're unsure — that song lyrics, like poetry, are a closed box, a mystery you can never entirely resolve. You think — although again you're unsure — that you *can* choose who to love, but it doesn't really matter.

You keep walking. You're not familiar with the house, you don't know if someone lives here or if it's just a holiday rental. You got invited so you're there, trying to work out where the song is coming from.

You follow the chords and you soon find yourself in the living room. You see several sofas, spread out. It's such a spacious room that the lights from outside barely lighten the darkness, but you make out a phone connected to an audio system. It's the only sign of activity in the room.

The day's heat is yet to drop; it's bound to your skin. Time, like a worm, shuffles past. Tonight feels like the slowest night of the whole summer. The notes suspend you in the air, solitary, melancholy, like flying saucers. You approach the phone, you pick it up, and a voice surprises you.

'Don't change the song.'

You turn around, stunned. You drop the device.

'Sorry.'

A figure emerges from one of the sofas. She had been lying down. Now she's sitting up. She's blonde, dressed for the day: cut-off shorts and a wide- necked white T-shirt.

'I was listening to it,' she says.

'I didn't realise … I didn't want to bother you.'

You can't make out her features, just her slender arms and bare feet.

'No problem.'

She huffs, and tucks her hair behind her ears.

She asks you, 'What were you going to put on?'

'Huh? Oh, erm, nothing.'

She remains silent. You remain silent. Facing each other a few metres apart. You wonder if you ought to leave. Maybe you should. But you don't.

'To be honest, I like this song,' you say.

'Really?'

'I heard it outside. That's why I came in.'

She stands up. She's not as tall as you thought. Nothing about her is particularly exuberant. And yet every curve, even the most subtle, leads beautifully to the next. You walk over to her, stopping about a metre away. Her eyes, even in the dimness, are a gleaming blue.

'Were you looking for someone?'

You suddenly feel as if you're on the edge of a great cliff, as if something decisive is about to happen. It's your stomach. It's a drop of sweat on your neck. It's a need to do something with your hands although you're not sure what.

'I'm not sure.' You smile. You put your hands in the pockets of your shorts. 'I thought it might be better in here than out there.'

'That's very optimistic of you.'

What's happening is a mystery. What does she make of you? You think that touching her skin would be like stroking a petal of a flower.

'This is one of Catupecu's best songs,' you say, if nothing else just to continue the conversation. You're rambling, but you don't know how to avoid it.

'Hmmm, I'm not sure it's their best. It's a cover of a song by—'

'Spinetta, I know.'

You surprised her. Just a little. A tiny flicker betrays her. Something in her look, a minute, involuntary pause.

'So,' you go on, 'are you staying nearby?'

'For a few days.'

She turns, sits back down and starts to pull on her shoes. Her sandals are beige, one strap around the ankle and another that runs down between her big toe and the next one along. Her nails are painted red. The movement is so sensual that your mind goes blank. She's not even doing anything special. Just the simple act of slipping on her sandals has become something extraordinary.

'Which version do you prefer?' she asks you, waking you from your stupor.

'This one,' you respond. 'What about you?'

'Why choose just one if I can have both?'

She stands up.

'You're leaving?' you enquire.

'Yes,' she replies. 'The song's finished.'

'Oh.'

You swallow as she moves towards the door.

'I can put it on again,' you say.

'No need.'

'Do you need me to come with you?'

Seriously? you think. *Did you really just say that, you superhero? Fool! You're such a fool.*

84

'Do you think I'm in danger?' comes her reply. The irony comes across in the last word. You deserve that, you think. And you don't know how to reply. She smiles like the Mona Lisa.

'Anyway,' she continues, 'who wants to live wrapped up in cotton wool all the time? Everyone else can look after me if they want to.'

And yes, she's going. Without so much as a backwards glance. She walks past you and keeps going.

'Don't forget your phone,' you say.

'It's not mine. It was just here.'

'What's your name?'

She doesn't stop, but she glances at you. Hesitates.

'Ask me another one.'

You smile, surprised.

'Will we meet again?'

'I don't know. You're the optimist.'

She exits the living room and walks through the doorway to the outside. You watch her moving away, as if the window is a cinema screen. You watch and you watch, until she disappears behind some trees in the street. You don't know it then — not yet — that something so trivial can lead to something so radical.

Back in the winter, you walk with your hands stuffed in your pockets, your gaze glued to the ground. In your ears, Catupecu sing words by Spinetta, where someone returns to search for someone else, but there's nothing left but the wind.

You agree, there's nothing but the wind. Yet right there, in the coldness of the empty street, in the frozen breath of

Irun, you're with her again. You and Lucrecia, Lucrecia and you. Alone. Because you imagine her with you, you imagine conversations with her, you imagine her indifference. Now she's here with you, with her perfume, unspeaking, and the two of you walk a while. You take a deep breath. You walk with her in silence, no need to say anything. There is no need for anything else.

Beyond your thoughts, in the real world, the air turns silver. Tiny snowflakes fall from the dark sky, something so perfectly white arriving from something so perfectly black. You contemplate the snow silently, more and more snowflakes arriving. The falling snow begins to erase Lucrecia's look, she bobs among the flakes. One by one she disappears.

'I've never seen snow before,' you tell her. It's the truth, but she no longer hears you.

The snow mixes with your clothing. You walk a while longer in silence, not even hearing the sound of your footsteps. In the gaps in the clouds, a few stars sparkle, and the scent of the snowy mountaintops descends towards you like a gale. Again, as if at the movies, you see the boy dressed as Death. He's now retracing his path, his parents behind him. He leaps along, enraptured in his own world of castles and pumpkins. He blows an endless stream of bubbles from a wand, a trail of transparent spheres that float in the air, fly towards the sky, dance, before disappearing in an inaudible and invisible explosion.

In the station, languages float in the air and tourists trudge by with suitcases, all of them fixed on their destinations, full of purpose and certainty about themselves: their lives determined by purchasing a ticket, checking the time, counting bags, finding the right seat.

You look at the clock on the station wall. A brief turn of the hands and it'll be midnight; the train will depart. You look around you. Again, the hubbub of faces, necks, bags and dust. You feel the remnants of nausea in your belly. You search for somewhere to sit down. You're exhausted. You buy a small bottle of water and take a few sips.

With a sigh, your fingers brush your stomach. Your head no longer hurts, and your body obeys you once again. Your body is your only home. It's your mansion, your palace. You take out your phone, connect to the station Wi-Fi and you're surprised to find a message from Lucrecia.

Lucrecia. Writing to you. Out of the blue. She doesn't tell you where she is. Or what she's thinking about. But she does ask how you are.

You blink as you re-read the message, studying the letters as if they are otherworldly. The *How are you?* seems too big, so vast, so endless, so inhuman that you don't even think of replying. Not even a single word.

You put your phone away again and stand up. You focus on the announcements board. It's not hard to find your train; it's the only one leaving Irun at this time. You walk towards the platform. The air is cold, still. The passengers, for the most part silent, are already boarding. Clouds of vapour escape from their nostrils.

Over the loudspeakers is a boarding call for passengers to Madrid. It almost seems a shame to leave. You get an irresistible urge to tell Lucrecia.

Perhaps that's what she was thinking about. Maintaining such a link, every so often. Connecting from time to time. Knowing that the other is somewhere on the planet. Maybe she wasn't pulling away from you but starting something new. Something you will have to discover along the way.

You look at the message again, incredulous, wondering if it's a mistake. And finally, you smile.

When the time comes to fight for her, you'll decide. But for now, it's enough to think that you might just be willing to do so.

You move ahead towards the dark carriages. You board without looking back. A mass of people squeeze together, looking for their places, pushing past you, propelling you forward, but you finally reach your seat. It's empty. This one is most definitely yours. Your mind's still thinking about Lucrecia's face, about how she smiled at you the first time you met. You look for her in the window. It's an irrational thing to do, senseless. You want to find her again among the snowflakes. But of course, she's not there. A strange, secret feeling of sadness settles in your chest.

'Beautiful snow, eh?' someone next to you remarks.

It's a lady with white hair, of indeterminable age and with blue eyes that are starting to fade. She asks you to help her with one of her bags. You're happy to oblige and she sits down next to you, in the aisle seat. She's going to accompany you all the way to Madrid, you can sense it.

'Yes,' you murmur.

She gives you a maternal smile, settling herself in, without unsettling you.

'Are you travelling?' she asks. She must have noticed your accent, but you're fine with it.

'Yes.'

'Alone?'

'Yes.'

'How brave! Aren't you scared?'

'No,' you reply. 'I like meeting new people.'

She smiles.

'How lovely. Well, I hope you meet a lot.'

It's your turn to smile now.

'Yes. So do I.'

You take out your ticket from your wallet, and search for something to listen to on your phone. You choose 'Loving Cup' by the Rolling Stones. Why not? You crank up the volume. The piano plays, Mick's voice floats in over the top and then the guitar comes in. The train begins to move. You look at Irun with the melancholy of goodbye.

And this is how you close your eyes, slowly, enjoying the knowledge of where you're going, even if you don't know exactly who you are.

Because, really, who are you?

Federico Ivanier © Alessandro Maradei recortada